D0764557

Grandma's Bill

MARTIN WADDELL

illustrated by

JANE JOHNSON

UNLV LIBRARY

WITHDRAWN

ORCHARD BOOKS
New York

X
PZ
W334 Gr

For Sally Doran—M.W.

For Darrell—J.J.

Text copyright © 1990 by Martin Waddell
Illustrations copyright © 1990 by Jane Johnson
First American Edition 1991 published by Orchard Books
First published in Great Britain by Simon & Schuster Young Books
All rights reserved. No part of this book may be reproduced or transmitted in any form or by any means, electronic or mechanical, including photocopying, recording or by any information storage or retrieval system, without permission in writing from the Publisher.

ORCHARD BOOKS
A division of Franklin Watts, Inc., 387 Park Avenue South, New York, NY 10016

Manufactured in the United States of America. Printed by
General Offset Company, Inc. Bound by Horowitz/Rae. Book design by Jean Krulis.

10 9 8 7 6 5 4 3 2 1

The text of this book is set in 18 pt. WTC Goudy Regular.
The illustrations are watercolors.

Library of Congress Cataloging-in-Publication Data
Waddell, Martin. Grandma's Bill / Martin Waddell.—1st American ed. p. cm. Summary: Grandma shows little Bill her photograph album with pictures of his grandfather, also named Bill. ISBN 0-531-05923-5. ISBN 0-531-08523-6 (lib. bdg.) [1. Grandfathers—Fiction.] I. Title. PZ7.W1137Gr 1991 [E]—dc20 90-43014

Every Thursday Bill went to see his grandma.

"Who is this?" said Bill.
"That's my Bill," Grandma said.
"*I'm* your Bill," said Bill, because he was.
"That's my other Bill," said Grandma.
"What other Bill?" asked Bill.
"Your daddy's daddy," said Grandma.
"I didn't know Daddy had a daddy,"
said Bill.
"Well, he did," said Grandma.

"Look, here's my book of photographs. That's Bill,"
Grandma said.
"That's a baby!" said Bill.

"He was a baby, to begin with," said Grandma.
"That's his mommy and daddy."
"They look funny!" said Bill.

"That's Bill again," Grandma said.
"He's not a baby anymore," said Bill.
"He's a big boy like you," said Grandma.
"I'm a little bigger," said Bill.

"Look at him now," said Grandma.
"He has funny knees!" said Bill.
"He wore shorts," said Grandma.
"I've got long pants," said Bill,
and he showed her.
"So you do," said Grandma.

"He's grown-up in this picture,"
said Grandma.
"Is that him?" asked Bill.
"That's Bill," said Grandma.
"And guess who that is!"

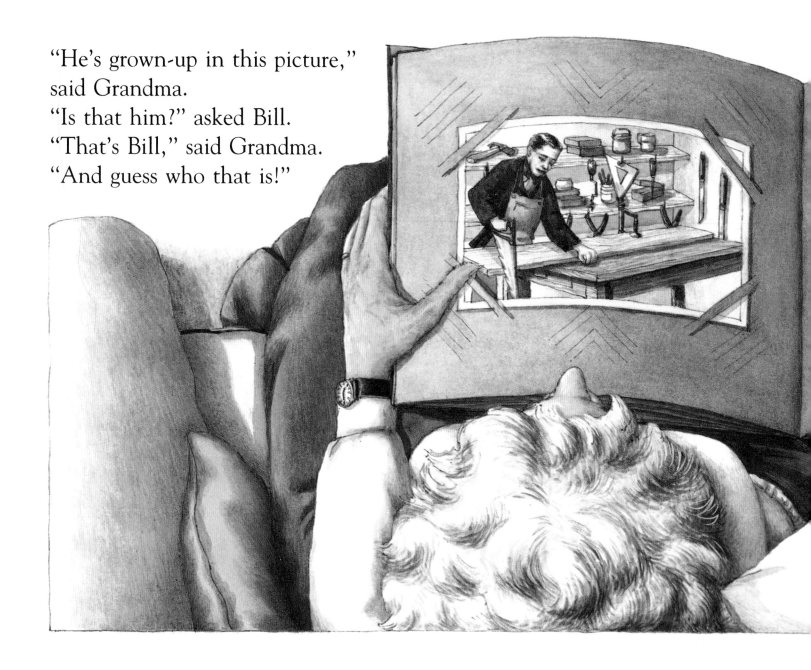

"Who is it?" said Bill.
"Me!" said Grandma.
"No, it's not," said Bill.
"*You*'re all wrinkled!"

"That's us getting married," said Grandma.
"Where are your wrinkles?" asked Bill.
"I didn't have any wrinkles then," said Grandma.
"You don't look right without them,"
said Bill.

"That's Bill in the army," said Grandma.
"That soldier?" Bill asked.
"Yes," said Grandma. "He fought in the war."
"Why?" said Bill.
"There was a big war," Grandma said.
"Lots of people fought in it."

"Guess who this one is?" said Grandma.
"Who?"
"That's your daddy. That's him with Bill
on the beach when he was a baby.
Your daddy was my baby," Grandma said.

"Who's that boy?" said Bill.
"That's your daddy, a little bigger," said Grandma. "And Bill."

"Why does Bill have a cane?" asked Bill.
"He was hurt in the war," said Grandma.

"My daddy's not in this one," said Bill.
"Yes, he is!" said Grandma. "That's him."
"Where's Bill?" Bill asked.

"Bill was working that day," said Grandma.
"Look at your hat!" said Bill.

"That's your daddy going to school," said Grandma.
"And that's Bill!" said Bill.
"Right," said Grandma.

"That's your daddy in his first job," said Grandma.
"But who's she?" asked Bill.
"You know who that is!" said Grandma.
"No, I don't," said Bill.

"That's your mommy," said Grandma.

"They look funny getting married," said Bill.
"People do," said Grandma.
"Is that you in that hat again?" said Bill.
"Yes," said Grandma.
"Why is Bill in that funny chair?" asked Bill.
"His legs didn't work right," said Grandma.

"That's OUR HOUSE!" shouted Bill.
"And me and your mommy and Bill," said Grandma.

"But where's my daddy?"
"I think he slept in!" Grandma answered.

"Where's *me*?" said Bill.
"You come in soon."

"There I am!" cried Bill.
"Yes," said Grandma.

"But where's Bill?" said Bill.
"Bill wasn't there anymore,"
said Grandma.

"Did he die?" Bill asked.
"Yes," said Grandma. "He did."

"I bet my daddy was sad," said Bill.
"Everybody was," said Grandma.
"It's all right, though, isn't it?" said Bill.
"Of course it is," said Grandma.

"You've still got a Bill," said Bill.
"I've still got *two* Bills," said Grandma.
"Where's the other one?" Bill asked.
"In my book," said Grandma.
And she closed the photo album
and put it back on the shelf.